WI[illegible]

'Sparse, poetic an[illegible]
three narrators in remote Sweden as they [illegible]
to find meaning in a rapidly changing world. An understated, powerful fable about the power of nature, this is a compact seed of a book, one that keeps growing long after you've finished it.'
Danielle Giles, author of *Mere*

'Turner's translation deftly captures the extraordinary density of feeling in these spare pages. This is a book that continues to resonate far beyond its final lines.' Rowe Irwin, author of *The Life Cycle of a Moth*

'Startling and rich'
Lucy Rose, author of *The Lamb*

'Hannah Lutz's novel is an allegory of humanity's plight in the age of impending climate catastrophe.'
Sydsvenskan

'In this thin little book, every page bursts with the paradoxes that surround man and nature today'
Expressen (Sweden)

THE EMMA PRESS

The Danish translation of *Vildsvin* was first published in 2016 by Rosinante in Denmark. The original Swedish text was first published in 2017 by Förlaget in Finland and Albert Bonniers Förlag in Sweden.

First published in the UK in 2025 by The Emma Press Ltd

Edited by James Trevelyan.

ISBN 978-1-915628-38-1

A CIP catalogue record of this book is available from the British Library.

Printed and bound in the UK by CMP Digital Print Solutions, Poole.

theemmapress.com
hello@theemmapress.com
Birmingham, UK

EU GPSR Authorised Representative
LOGOS EUROPE, 9 rue Nicolas Poussin,
17000, LA ROCHELLE, France
E-mail: Contact@logoseurope.eu

This book has been selected to receive financial assistance from English PEN's PEN Translates programme, supported by Arts Council England. English PEN exists to promote literature and our understanding of it, to uphold writers' freedoms around the world, to campaign against the persecution and imprisonment of writers for stating their views, and to promote the friendly co-operation of writers and the free exchange of ideas.
www.englishpen.org

ENGLISH PEN FREEDOM TO WRITE FREEDOM TO READ

ARTS COUNCIL ENGLAND Supported using public funding by ARTS COUNCIL ENGLAND

wild boar

a novel

hannah lutz

translated from swedish
by andy turner

THE EMMA PRESS

Ritve

I have seen them, the wild boar, they have found their way into my dreams! Now I know the way they move, the sounds they make when they sneak into the gardens. I have to listen carefully to hear their trotters and snouts in the grass. They are so numerous, so solid, and yet they make such light work of quietly moving around, it's incredible. Here I am, heavy and warm with sleep. I open the curtains, see the sea. The sheets on the bed are white.

This is what I know of Hornanäs: to get there I will make my way to Småland, to Tingsryd, and midway between Tingsryd and Linneryd I'll turn right. In the village there are four or five occupied houses, three or four abandoned ones. In a yellow house, surrounded by apple trees, lives Arnold Falkberg. The landscape is made up of lakes and productive forest. Wild boar hunting is permitted throughout the year.

Arnold Falkberg often has a camera with him when he is in the forest. Many people film wild boar, most focusing on the hunting. I've seen the clips they post on YouTube. In a Swedish Television documentary, Arnold Falkberg is known as *The Hunter of Hornanäs*, his hunting rifle propped against the armchair during the interview. But now I've seen the footage he's posted, I don't believe he's fired a shot at a single wild boar in his life. The hand holding that camera is intent on something completely different.

I was so moved by the films that I bought a ticket from Finland in the middle of high season. I'm sitting on the sun deck watching the islands drift by, the Stockholm archipelago and its terraces and towers, so quaint, a warm embrace. The people on the islands have woken up and are lying on rocks and jetties reading. We sail by, eclipsing their morning sun for a moment. Passengers on deck are waving at the shore and taking photos. Some people turn their faces to the ship, waving back.

Glenn

The project proposals roll into the local council at a steady pace; I sit in the office opening letters and emails. I read, observing: history repeats itself, ideas flourish, die, are forgotten, until they reappear as new. The applications speak to the mood of our times. Their language is energetic. I don't read them particularly thoroughly, saying yes to the majority. I don't listen to the news any more – I've heard it all before. Instead I try to listen to Tove's podcast where she and her friends comment on the news and present their own. But it's so trendy, and everything happens somewhere else, in other countries, or in Malmö or Gothenburg; there's very little to say about Tingsryd local district. I can live with that. I don't regret moving. I'd like to stay here, going about my everyday life. I compost and darn my old socks though I know we're heading for a new Ice Age. I read somewhere that prevailing climatic conditions can at most be called an intermediate period, and Ice Ages are the normal state of affairs. One day, perhaps soon, a wind will sweep in across the terrain causing people in the northern hemisphere to freeze on the spot. We won't have time to ready ourselves – it'll happen without warning. I've resigned myself to the idea: it will all indeed end in some way. I have no God, no children, don't want eternal life. I go to work, read the applications and distribute council money. It's okay – I do it with a light touch. I'm home by quarter past four, make coffee, listen to music, prepare dinner or tidy up while I wait for Martina. Her work demands more mental engagement than mine. She comes home emotionally exhausted and when she's late she's starving, she throws her arms around me saying, Glenn, I'm starving! She's the best company when she's starving. She eats in a state of rapture, in huge mouthfuls, chatting in long, incomplete sentences. She drinks copious amounts of wine without getting drunk. I drink less but get tipsy, laugh at my own bad jokes and try to get her talking about her clients. In our early days together she'd get indignant, seeing it as a lack of respect for her work. Now she just brushes it aside or makes something up, telling tall tales. It's easy to hear if she's spinning a yarn, but I love all her fictitious clients, their moods and quirky relationships with each other, their crises, her interest in them.

Mia

We're staying in the summer rooms of the building's south wing. The school is called Siggalycke. Sigga-lycke. I sent an application in to Tingsryd local council – I called the project *Recollections of a Sigga Child,* the first contribution to a sound archive in Tingsryd's local heritage museum. I have no doubt that Grandad will find his voice again, given the right circumstances. It can't be that hard. We're going to be children again, I said to Grandad, we're going to be Sigga kids. He pretended not to hear.

The reply from the council arrived a week later. A building, the Siggalycke Elementary School itself, was at our disposal. They called it a *residency grant.* Sara was reading the letter over my shoulder.

What are you doing? she said.

We're going to Siggalycke.

I thought you were joking, she said.

We'll be staying for the summer.

It's not your fault.

Stop it, I said.

But it isn't, she said, don't you see? There's nothing you can do. He's old. People get old.

She took my hand.

No, I said. Not like this.

He needs peace and quiet, she said. He needs to be somewhere they can look after him.

You don't get it, I said. He needs me.

We arrived on the fifteenth of June. Glenn Vester from the local council met us on the steps and showed us around. We had a cup of coffee and talked about the geothermal heating system and the well-preserved classrooms. Glenn was looking at Grandad with interest.

He's a bit shy, I said.

Glenn nodded kindly.

In the hall he thanked us for coming – it meant a lot for the local area. And, I mean, it's good for the building to be lived in, he said.

It took me several days to get used to Siggalycke. Grandad mostly kept himself to the kitchen, continuing to behave as if it were just any old place. I walked around the rooms and listened to them, knocking on the walls. Here. This is where the Sigga children lived. This is where they sat, for days on end. They hung on the wall bars. Autumn, winter, spring. This is where they yanked each other's hair and threw each other's school bags into the brook. This is where they grew up and turned into teenagers, growing big clumsy bodies and hair under their arms. Grandad too.

Oh, to be a Sigga child, that was something special! I learned that early on. Grandad used to sit in his armchair in the corner and talk long into the night. Afterwards I would lie awake. I used to think about the Sigga children, about the schoolhouse, why they called it that, Sigga-lycke, Sigga's fortune. I wanted to know what it looked like. I wanted to have maps and Grandad would draw outlines, labelling all the rooms. The small hall. The big hall. The equipment room. The library. The workshop. The larder. My best friend Rava and I studied the maps, got to know the building like our own, all the little crannies you could hide in, the dark corners and splendid botanical paintings on the walls. We played Siggalycke. In our games Grandad was our age and we were his friends. We squabbled over who got to be Ivar Sandberg, the schoolmaster who taught Grandad everything he knows. Ivar Sandberg loved taking a stroll at night, Grandad used to tell us. Ivar Sandberg could see in the dark, we said. He would dream while he was strolling, Grandad said. Ivar Sandberg never slept! we said. We would dress up in Grandad's old shirts and caps. Every night Ivar Sandberg would walk around the various rooms, we said, seeing to things around the building, dealing with the pupils, checking they were fine, that they had blankets and were dreaming happy dreams as they slept on the floor of the gymnasium. No, no, we didn't sleep at school, Grandad said. In the morning he would wake them with merry music and songs, we said. The schoolmaster was particularly interested in botany, Grandad told us, and we learned the Latin names for dandelion and wood anemone so we could sound like Ivar Sandberg when we talked about nature. Oh, taraxacum officinale! we shouted to each other.

And then there was the wild boar game. We could only play it outdoors at night, so we didn't always dare. But when we did, it was deadly serious. In the game Ivar Sandberg goes for his nightly stroll in the garden, where he meets a lone wild boar called Sigga. Wild boar always move in a sounder, something Ivar Sandberg knows, so he stands perfectly still, waiting for the rest of them. When they fail to appear, he sits beneath a tree. Sigga comes up to him, saying all the wild boar in the world apart from her have died from a horrible disease inflicted by humans. Without her sounder, she sees no sense in life. She has come to Siggalycke to lie beneath her favourite tree and die.

Ivar Sandberg answers her in different ways. Sometimes with a great understanding silence. Sometimes with an invitation to the human herd. I can only be happy with my own kind, answers Sigga. You were the ones who took my kin. Now you want me. To turn me into a mascot. You're mistaken there, says Ivar Sandberg, you shall have your own desk and your own pens and rubbers. You shall sleep in the gymnasium under blankets with the children and learn about plants and foreign countries.

The game always ends with Sigga lying down next to Ivar Sandberg beneath the tree and both of them falling asleep. When Ivar Sandberg wakes up, he realises it is the first time he has ever slept, and that Sigga is dead.

Ritve

The final driver of the day is called Kamal.

You're old, he says to me.

Am I? I say.

You look old.

I'm nearly forty, I say.

Yes, that's old, he says. We're both old.

Night is falling and the road is wide and bright. We sit in silence with the windows open, swishing through the clouds of insects, crushing them against the windscreen at 120 km/h. Here comes death, a white two-door Honda Civic with automatic transmission. Kamal drops me off at a petrol station east of Linköping. He will drive on, around Lake Vättern, via Gothenburg and on again, driving all night but going in the wrong direction.

Are you sure you don't want to tag along? All the way to Trollheimen, it's heaven on earth! I shake my head. Safe journey, we say to each other. He zooms off. I go into the petrol station and buy coffee, sit down at the hot dog counter and watch the telly. The morning papers arrive. I get a lift with the newspaper driver to the next petrol station; we drag the bundles inside and she drives away. I take a seat on a bench outside. When I close my eyes, I can hear the morning traffic down on the E4 motorway.

Glenn

Very little land came with the house. The forest around us is owned by big business and business transforms the landscape from day to day. The trees are being felled in great swathes to create space for new ones to be planted.

This is where they were born – my grandmother, grandfather, their forefathers – and where they lived and died. And so it continues. Or it begins again. It could be called returning to your roots. However, no one around here remembers my relatives. Their houses were small and looked like all the others – the sum of their lives left no obvious traces behind. Tingsryd – not the most beautiful local district in Sweden. There is something reassuring in that. And this, too, is something to love. Here I am on the grass, far from Malmö. Fanning off the sweat and scratching my chest. It is cool and partly cloudy, wind from the southeast, I have woken early, already mown the lawn. Martina is still in bed. Saturday and three weeks to the holidays. The garden is already heavy with foliage, and moisture from the night still lingers. I don't want to say anything to Martina, but I'm starting to feel something. She would call it *the connection*, which she has been waiting for. It's coming, she says. Pah! I say. I get tired thinking about the connection. That's not what I'm feeling, it's not the sense of belonging to my kin and history, but something else, something lighter. Fields and lakes, vast and desolate, monotonous forests extending in all directions. Here I'm nobody special, just whoever you like, roaming the local area – keeping up with the changes in the landscape, the work in the forest and the big gravel pit, full of water, clear and transparent, turquoise like the Mediterranean.

I think it must be warm too. I saw someone swimming there.

Ritve

The Canadian city of Winnipeg has more sleepwalkers than any other place on earth. I saw a film about Winnipeg, about the sleepwalkers – *we dream of where we walk, and walk to where we dream*. In sleep we are lost, or in sleep we know what we want. We want to go home. We make for home, to our old addresses. That is why the citizens of Winnipeg always carry a bunch of keys to their old homes. They have got used to accommodating each other's sleepwalking – the stranger on the couch is left to sleep in peace until they wake up and find their way quietly out of the house. People don't ask; everyone knows, everyone recognises it, the lure, the sleep mantra – *old dreamy addresses, old dreamy addresses*. Through the snow and the avenues, fully dressed, wearing inevitable death and inevitable life like an oppressive heat beneath your coat. Home now, before it's too late – or it's already too late – so home, where else can you go, home. They are all so tired, so tired. They want to get away from Winnipeg, from all the snow, from all the old addresses they drag around with them like suitcases, heavier and heavier. They board the train heading out of town, but they always fall asleep, always fall asleep as the train moves along its lulling, cradling track through all the other towns and back to Winnipeg. When they wake up, they are somehow always back in Winnipeg.

Glenn

A sounder of wild boar walked through our plot overnight. I woke up at a quarter to three feeling hungry and got out of bed. I saw the wild boar from the window on the stairs as I went down to the kitchen. My first thought was to wake Martina, but I couldn't take my eyes off them. Sometimes they dig up our lawn but now they were just walking over it, perfectly calmly, and vanishing into the edge of the forest. I went into the kitchen and heated up what was left from dinner. I ate slowly and stayed at the table after I had finished. I wanted a coffee. I made coffee and had a cup, then another one. The sun came up. I put out the breakfast and splashed my hair under the kitchen tap, sat at the table and buttered a slice of bread. The sun just goes on shining.

Mia

Grandad needs some fresh air, fuck the rain. We take cover beneath the dripping trees. We walk down the path. I take his hand. Our wellies squelch in the moss. I wipe the snot and rain off my face. I ask him what the mushrooms are called. I point to them one after another. Keep talking, Mia, keep talking. I keep talking. I feel stupid. I pretend to be more stupid than I am. Grandad, what's a death cap? He must hate me. I mean, we're both adults now. Is this love, or is it murder? Am I the one who is ultimately destroying him? The more I speak, the further he moves out of sight. I walk by his side, tending to him. Grandad, you can live through my strong body. He hardly looks at the mushrooms. I don't know if he is cold in the rain. I have wrapped a big yellow raincoat around him. He isn't wearing it, he is just underneath it. I have a small tape recorder with me just in case – you never know if he might start talking. Here I am, fumbling with the recorder, trying to protect it from the rain, taping all the sounds around me that are not Grandad. What do I think I'm doing? What is the use in me crying? Is this *love?*

I dry Grandad's hair. I dry my own hair. I blow my nose, take a seat in the kitchen. I bite my nails. Fucking Sara. Where is she now? What is she doing? She is listening to the rain on the skylight in a flat that is suddenly full of peace. She is happy, will come up with something soon, start making money. She'll probably be famous. She's good at so many things.

The months Grandad stayed with us were unbearable. What for Sara was the unbearable presence of Grandad was the unbearable lack of Grandad's presence for me. How Grandad was faring, who the hell even knew, but it was better than being at The Birches care home. Of course, Sara didn't think so. But what did she know, she never showed any interest, he was just old, he said nothing, what was there to be interested in? Now Sara is living in the lap of luxury. She has packed up his stuff in the little case and put it in the cupboard. She smokes in bed, leaving all the windows open so the wind can blow away the smell of Grandad.

The last night in the flat we had sex in a way we'd never tried before. Cold and hard, like strangers. I think it was something she wanted to teach me. Now when I masturbate, I always think of that time.

Ritve

The grey sow is the biggest, she is the matriarch of the sounder. She knows every spot of grass in the countryside, the slopes and farms; the others follow her quietly trotting through the pine forest. It is night, the noises are muffled, she stops, raising her snout to the sky. They approach the wetlands, she wants to swim. She senses the damp earth in the air and leads the sounder out across the meadow, down the hillside, there, to where the water is visible between the tree trunks. Down to the shore. The little ones are to swim as well. The sows enter the water and the boarlets wag their tails, standing at the water's edge waiting. The large sow has swum far away from the others, now she turns back and swims towards the land. She comes out of the water and rolls in the mud on the shoreline, shaking herself over the boarlets, nudges them lightly with her snout. They yield and slip into the water. They snort. It is morning. I'm pounding like a big new heart.

The local bed and breakfast has a warm, light dining room and homemade bread. I fill my plate and my pockets, I sit down at a window. Thin fabrics, curtains and tablecloths in airy colours, people sitting at some of the tables. I want to tell them about the dream, but they're busy doing their own thing, chattering among themselves or reading the papers. When they stretch, the fine hairs on their arms shine in the sunlight. In the mornings I sometimes find myself filled with an intense yearning for them, the other people, their soft arms and legs, their faces not yet hardened by the day. I want to caress them with my hands before my own fingers grow hard too.

I lie on the bed for a while, digesting breakfast. I look up to the skylight and the yellow curtains. Clear my throat, test my voice, hello, hello there, saying a few phrases aloud. I am ready to see Arnold Falkberg. Yesterday he wasn't at home, which was just as well. I'd become uneasy, regretting it as soon as I'd knocked on the door. The neighbour was curious and introduced himself, wanting to talk. I just said hello and hurried back to my B&B.

I don't envisage a particularly spectacular meeting. Just a series of informal conversations with Arnold Falkberg before I set off for the forest myself. Tips from one enthusiast to another, practical advice, a few anecdotes maybe. I get up slowly and look at myself in the mirror. Adjust my shirt and comb my hair, walk out into the hall, down the old, crooked staircase and through the rooms. I nod to some of the guests on the veranda. I stroll along the road, through the forest, around the lengthy bend and past the barns at the turn-off for Hornanäs. Up along the path. I carry on to Falkberg's house and knock at the door. The car is parked close to the house and a little robot is moving around cutting the grass. The neighbour, Per Anders, is sitting on a plastic chair next door; he says good morning and that Arnold Falkberg is home, he was out bright and early collecting his newspaper. I knock one more time and wait. Watch the robot at work. It seems very quiet in the house and the curtains are drawn in two of the rooms. Perhaps he is sitting inside watching his films. Or perhaps he is mostly awake at night when the wild boar are moving about. That would be a reasonable assumption. I sit down on the grass. The ground is swaying. It is the Baltic Sea. I lurch with the waves.

Glenn

The embers are perfect now. I've been stoking the fire all day; the old stone oven in the outhouse is smoking. The pizza only needs five minutes and we dive into it while waiting for the next one. I can see Martina is impressed: I never thought we'd get a fire going in there, she says. We soon satisfy our hunger but we can't stop eating. I want to make the most of the heat. I roll out the last of the dough and decorate it with tomatoes and olives. Martina pours wine into my glass and kisses my neck; I continue to stare into the embers. We should do this more often, she says. You're lovely, Glenn. I close the oven door and sit beside her on the bench. She smells of sweet pepper and melted cheese. I want to have sex right there on the bench, feel the rough wood scraping up against my back, Martina's hair in my eyes. I drink the last of the wine from my glass, turning towards her. It's ready now, I say. She nods. I stand up and open the oven door. The heat hits me in the face and I quickly take the pizza to the table. Martina has got to her feet and is making her way out to the garden. No, I say, come here. I pull her towards me. Unbutton my trousers, I say. Lay me on the bench. She guides me down onto my back, moving her hands up to my face. Your cheeks are red hot, you're so beautiful, she says. Sit on me, I say. Kiss me.

Ritve

The heat arrives with the rain; I only have a thin t-shirt on under my raincoat. I walk along the path into the woods north of Arnold's house, passing time. I close my eyes, stretching my arms towards the trees. *We sleep as we walk, walk as we dream*. In the rain everything is close, familiar. I can almost sense the melody of old addresses. The names, the parishes, Siggalycke, Björnehult, Hornanäs, Hornanäs. How much time, how much time does it take to turn into a sleepwalker, how many times must I repeat myself in order to create a pattern? This is where the wild boar became a part of the fauna again. Here, on this barren, stony soil where they were once driven to extinction, they were re-introduced and fenced-in some hundred years later by a baron with a hunting lodge. A nice complement to the meagre hares and deer, once again a natural part of the forests of Sweden. The wild boar want to leave Småland, want to get away from home, but to no avail: they only go around in circles. Every night to the same wooden fences, rooting in the same old soil. Is it the dreams keeping them there? The sleep? *And as we walk to where we dream, we are always lost, befuddled. Why are we so sleepy? Why can't we just open our eyes?* I open my eyes, undo my coat and air my chest.

Glenn

My mobile is flashing: it's Tove. I rush out into the coffee room – Tove! We haven't spoken for months, I've only heard her voice on her podcast, where it sounds harder, older, like someone I don't recognise. She's just phoning quickly, she explains. She's coming to visit on Saturday, if we're at home. I'm thrilled, laughing down the receiver. Tove! I thought you said you'd never come, I say. Ah, she says, well you can always change your mind.

Leaving Malmö wasn't hard, but leaving Tove was. Here we go, she said when we left, now you'll be like every other couple. I felt ashamed; Martina rolled her eyes. What about every other couple? she said. You know what I mean, Tove said.

The first few years Martina and I were together we would often babysit Tove at Martina and Tove's dad's place. Later, when she was grown up, she would stay with us when she didn't have anywhere of her own. Before Martina got home we would often sit in the kitchen for hours, reading papers and listening to music, preparing complicated dishes using all sorts of extravagant ingredients she'd scavenged from bins behind supermarkets. In the mornings she used to wake up early, frequently agitated, wanting to talk about the meaning of life, what the point of it all was. I tried to comfort her with the start of an Edith Södergran poem: *Be calm, my child, there is nothing, and everything is as you see: the forest, the smoke and the retreating rails.* No, she said, there has to be more than that. I tried to explain what I meant. Life is incomprehensible, I said, we understand so much less than we think. It's best to just let go, be here as best we can, accept it's meaningless, in a good way, that's what I think, I said. She scoffed at me. Bullshit, Glenn.

Ritve

I knock and wait, rattling the door handle up and down slightly. Locked. Per Anders calls me over and I walk across the grass. He is standing in the fading light beating posts into the ground. Time for some electric fences in Hornanäs! Look here, he waves his arms theatrically, the electrified wire runs at just the right height to catch their sensitive snouts! He straightens up and contemplates his work. It doesn't bother me that much, them rooting around here, he says. I'm mostly worried about the vegetables I've grown for the grandchildren. There's got to be something left, at least for a handful of salad when they arrive. He takes a seat on the chopping block and peers up at me. Have you seen those little red mushrooms? he says. Just down there by the forest. You haven't? They're quite special. Walk down and take a look. They have this almost unnatural glow in the half-light.

I pick up one of the clods of earth rooted up by the wild boar, weighing it in my hands. I place it back on the grass.

Mia

Grandad doesn't want to go out in the evenings. He resists when I try to put a coat on him after dinner, despite the almost white darkness of these days. We're going out to see Ivar Sandberg, I say. I'm tired of Grandad not reacting. I'm tired of talking to him as if we are talking to each other. Ivar! I shout. Ivar Sandberg! Grandad looks at me, and then at the kitchen light. Ivar Sandberg never sleeps, here we come! I shout out of the window. Ivar Sandberg! Grandad sits down at the table.

I go outside. I stand in the grounds. I walk up and down the grass a bit. I don't know if I enjoy being here. I don't know what to say about it. Siggalycke. This is where I am now, Sigga-lycke. And why doesn't he say anything? Why doesn't he want to do anything? It's all ours! We are Sigga children now! I shout SIGGA CHILDREN! SIGGA CHILDREN! I see him through the window. He's sitting there. Calm and quiet like at home. He can dress by himself, go to the toilet. He remembers where things are kept and how to make coffee. But nothing grabs his attention. And what about my attention? I feel empty when I look at the schoolhouse. I try to think of our games, to enter into them. Grandad in a cap and short trousers, the grass teeming with children. Rava and me. Hello, Ivar Sandberg! Hello, taraxacum officinale! Hello, old Sigga, where's the tree we buried you under, where we buried you a thousand times? White, white night. Is this what you look like?

Glenn

Tove ought to be here by now. She called when she was on the train to Växjö, but that was hours ago. She wanted to walk the last ten kilometres here, said she needed to be on her feet after such a long journey. Martina and I have been sitting on the couch forever. Martina, as usual, is reading her book and making notes in the margins. I stare out into the dusk, trying to hold it off. But time passes so quickly, it's almost dark.

It's almost dark, I say to Martina.

It doesn't get dark this time of year, she says without looking up.

Shouldn't I phone? I say.

She'll be in touch if she needs a lift.

Yes, but what if something's happened, I say.

Nothing's happened, she says.

I stand up.

It's been four hours since she called!

Martina puts her book down, she looks up at me.

She stands, putting her hands on my shoulders, hugging me. Glenn, look, here we go again. I sigh. She takes hold of my hands, looking right at me.

Glenn.

I nod. I know, I say. I know, I know.

Come and sit down, she says. She sits down. I remain on my feet, shaking my head.

I'm going for a drive, I say.

Martina looks at me for a long time. Shall I come too? she says.

No. I just have to get out for a bit.

I drive past the old elementary school. At this time of evening the grounds are wild and dreamy, and a figure is walking across the grass. I wonder what they are actually doing there. I don't remember what was in the application – I didn't manage to read it all. It's so rare for anyone to apply for residency grants and it's good for the building to be lived in, I was just glad to have them. I consider whether to look in one day, find out how things are.

I drive to the gravel pit, parking alongside one of the large mountains of grit. I stare at the water ahead through the windscreen. Shall I get out, dip my toes? Or just jump in, let the water flow through my hair? I drum on the steering wheel. I look at the time. I start the car and take the same route back home.

Ritve

I don't see the mushrooms. Maybe I'm too late and the light has changed. I go into the forest, walking along the tractor tracks. It's hard to imagine any wildlife here: the trees are in long, cultivated rows, the animal tracks have been swallowed up by the elastic moss. The forest floor is so different from the rocks by the sea. There, the traces left by animals are as clear as day, gull shit and eider feathers plastered to the stones, eggshells of different colours.

I lived in the outer archipelago for many years. I used to dream of bulkier animals than the ones I would meet on the rocks. The birds were bigger than I was when they extended their wings, but they were wily, could take to the air in an instant. Their size was never a burden on the ground.

Under the water I would train my own body for lightness. I would crawl along the bottom in the ooze, make an elegant leap upwards, grasping the water in my arms and launch myself to the surface up and over the rocks where the gulls and terns were waiting to flap away and land on other rocks. Then I would lie there on my stomach, heavy against the hot stones.

Once an elk swam out to the island; Aunt Zoya and I were brushing our teeth among the reeds when it came up onto the shore. It stood there motionless for a long time, glaring right ahead. When it saw us, it shook the water from its coat and tramped around in a circle, then it went back into the water again and swam away. The island is too small and rugged, Zoya said. It's off to find a forest.

When I return to Falkberg's house the light has grown thinner and, looking out from the illuminated garden, the forest is black. The bushes, the moss, the ferns, the stumps, even the long, straight rows of tree trunks form a compacted darkness that closes in around itself. It is hard imagining that I had been there just a moment ago, and hadn't blended into the forest. Per Anders is sitting on his veranda. I knock once more at Falkberg's door, but mostly out of force of habit. Per Anders beckons me over. I sit down next to him on the bench. He offers me a beer, insects swarming about the lights in the veranda ceiling. I button up my coat; the mosquitoes land on my shoulders and tiny gnats get caught in the hairs on my legs. We drink our beers.

So where are you staying? Per Anders asks.

At the bed and breakfast, I say.

You are, are you? he says.

It's nice, I say. But my money's almost spent. I'm going to buy a tent.

Per Anders nods. I blow a note across the top of my beer bottle.

I haven't camped out since I was a child, I say.

I've never camped out, he says. My brothers and sisters went to camp every summer. I was far too scared, he says.

Of what?

Everything.

He laughs.

And now I'm just too comfortable, he says. I'm not tempted.

We sit listening to the forest.

I down what's left from my bottle.

I dream about the wild boar, I say. Every night. I have done for several weeks.

He laughs, turning towards me.

You do, do you? he says.

And the biggest sow, I say, you should have seen her, last night she came close, she was almost twice my size, even though her legs are so short, and then they were all around me, and they touched me and yet they didn't, or they were –

I close my eyes, try again. They were – as if they were –

Ritve.

Per Anders places a hand on my shoulder.

I nod.

Ritve, he's here, Arnold.

I open my eyes, only just. Squint into the darkness. He is waving from down among the apple trees.

Per Anders, he calls, any news on your claim for the damp? Did they pay out?

Hey there, says Per Anders. There's someone here who'd like to see you.

Arnold Falkberg comes limping across the grass. He is smaller than I remember from the films; thinner, with a red beret and sloping shoulders beneath his large sweater.

I stand up.

I see, he says, and who do we have here?

He peers up at me.

Ritve. I saw the programme about you on TV.

I see, yes. Arnold Falkberg, hello there. He shakes my hand very lightly.

I'm a film-maker too, I say.

Nice to meet you, he says. And then: Yes, and I'm a hunter.

Your films, I say, they're amazing. I clear my throat. Really, amazing.

He laughs. He doesn't look at me, he looks at Per Anders. He says: Yes, yes, they are funny, the pigs. They are that, for sure.

Are there more films? I say.

Oh, he says, it was just for fun mostly.

I'd love to see more, I say. Or do you have any good tips? I'm also off into the forest.

I've left all that behind me, you see, he says.

The films?

You know, I've got other stuff to be getting on with. Don't have the time.

I see. But do you have any tips at all? How I can get close to them?

He laughs. Keep a cool head, he says. They're everywhere, see. Just keep a cool head.

Now he looks at me.

Good luck. Nice you're keeping busy with it.

He turns to Per Anders.

Mia

I'm restless, walking circles inside. Pacing up and down the big hall. There are pictures on the walls. I stop to look at them. I do another lap through the building. Back to the pictures. I attempt to stand still for a while though my legs are keen to keep moving. I look at an old class photo taken outside by the spruce hedge. The trees are young, spindly. The picture was taken in 1936: Grandad hadn't even started school, but when I stare at the children I feel I wouldn't have liked Grandad as a child. I feel we wouldn't have been friends at all. I can see it in my mind's eye. Grandad is standing in the water, with buck teeth and lank hair. He is pale. He can't swim. And we are shouting to him: *Stick-in-the-mud! Stick-in-the-mud!* He just stands there, moving neither his arms nor his legs. Keeping himself in the shallow end of the lake, far from the hollow where the rest of us compete to see who is brave enough to dive deepest. He stays in the water longer than we do, he knows we will pull his swimming trunks down as soon as he comes out. And it goes on – I can't stop the images. I see myself staying behind one morning after my dip, after the others have run off to school. I linger in the water with him. He looks at me with big, stupid eyes. I grab hold of him, force his head down below the surface to avoid seeing it, seeing his inadequacy. His arms and legs, usually so still under water, thrash and flounder. I hold him there, bearing down until his muscles stop twitching and his arms and legs regain their stillness, but in a new way, like seaweed, billowing.

Glenn

Glenn, Tove says, are you both actually going to stay here? She is lying on her stomach on the grass with her cheek on a cushion. I've retired to the shade of the garden swing chair. Tove is gleaming in the sun. Martina comes outside and sits next to Tove. She throws me a beer.

Is this where the two of you *live* now? Tove says.

She turns her head and looks at me.

Yes, I say, and open my beer. I look at Martina. She shrugs.

I'm not going anywhere, she says.

Shit, says Tove.

We never said we'd come back, I say.

No, she says. But I didn't think this was your kind of thing. I just thought this living in the countryside, I don't know, sure it's all lovely, but what's there to do here?

Martina nudges her. Aren't you moving here then? So something does happen?

I can't, you know that, it wouldn't work.

I raise my beer to her. We may just as well face the Ice Age here as anywhere else, I say.

Oh, the Ice Age! Tove sits up. That's around the corner, huh? So we get to avoid all the awkward questions?

I scratch the back of my neck and stare at my knees, irritated. I regret bringing it up. Tove gets up and sits next to me on the swing.

Sorry, she says.

Pah, I say.

The air is still. I brush a fly away. Tove positions her feet, and we swing back and forth above the grass.

Ritve

The saw is screeching, stacks of felled spruce and pine are everywhere. The trees are marked: they will be processed into paper and energy. This is no virgin forest, no jungle, but it's still extensive, dense, full of brushwood and scrub. And the wild boar have been here, rooting about everywhere. I pitch my tent among bushes and low trees and collect stones to make a fire pit. I plan my routes through the landscape.

I go on long walks, rest in my tent; it rains and the trees whisper. The cloud cover breaks and I find a patch of raspberries. It appears to belong to my neighbour, but Pah, she says, there are so many this year we can share them. She introduces herself: Gittan. Looks at me curiously. So, who are you? You don't look like you're from around here. But you speak good Swedish. Are you staying nearby? Yes, I say. For the time being anyway. I'm camping out. Oh, I see, she smiles.

We continue picking. I sense her looking at me from the side. What's your name, then? she asks after a while. Ritve. She nods. You're not drinking the water from the lakes, are you, Ritve? It's not pure, you know. No, you're to come to me, she points, my house is close by. There's water there, she explains, not that acid stuff that's normal around here, no. She has installed a new filter to regulate the pH value, it was expensive, but what a difference! She smiles. She has thick, dark eyebrows and a yellow anorak. We pick raspberries and I tell her I have made my way here to get close to the wild boar, to document them. She nods, saying: So are you mapping their spread?

No, I say, not exactly.

She frowns. But it's the hunt you're filming?

No, no, I say. Just the wild boar.

She is silent for a while. Then she says: They're a big problem. They trample over our fields and gnaw on the grains.

I nod. I saw it on film, I say.

They've spread very quickly, she says, there are so many of them this year. But they're probably hard to film, you know? They're clever and shy, especially the old sows. Moving at dusk and during the night. Did you bring a light?

A torch?

No, a camera light, she says, so you can film in the dark?

There's a setting, I say, night shot.

Yes, right, she says.

I pick a few raspberries, put them in my mouth and ponder for a while. I look at Gittan, who has already filled a small bucket with berries.

May I film you? I ask.

Me?

Yes, you have some experience with wild boar.

I see. Yes, well why not? Be my guest. She pushes her hair behind her ears. She smiles down into her raspberries. So, what should I say then?

I take the camera out of the case.

Can you tell me the bit about the fields again, about what happens?

I watch her through the lens.

Right, she scratches her forehead. Shall I look into the camera?

If you want.

She glances sideways.

Yes, well, she says, they're a big problem. They're so fond of wheat, you see. So fond of it.

Can you tell me about them? Who it is, eating your wheat?

She looks sternly into the camera.

The wild boar. They harvest the grains from our

fields before we get the chance to. We go outside and it's all gone. Gone! Can you imagine? All our work!

She looks out into the forest.

Well, I'm off home now. Can you, she waves her hand in front of the camera, can you turn it off?

I turn it off.

Great. Come over when you want some water then.

Mia

I'm scared. I can't sleep. Tomorrow is midsummer. I don't dare go out into the light. It's so empty in here! I'm lying under blankets, missing all the others. And the schoolhouse and the night are opening up in all directions. Where are the children? When are they coming? When are the children coming?

Glenn

I was thinking of going for a walk. Want to come along?

Tove looks up from her computer. She nods.

We walk for a long time, side by side, kicking tree cones and peering up at the birds.

I don't have anywhere to live, says Tove. They sold the house.

What? They realised you were living there?

I think they heard something from the neighbours. They never came out there themselves. I've no idea how they sold it! The roof's been leaking all through spring. Fucking shit. Such fucking crap.

Can't you stay with Madin? Or with what's his name, Torbjörn?

She shrugs, I don't know. Maybe for a few weeks. She picks up a stick from the path.

You know you can stay here, I say.

Well, yes, I know, but honestly though, what would I do? You both have your jobs and that. She snaps the stick in two. She looks up into the trees. But what would I do? If I were to live in the country, she says, then I'd live up in Norrland. Did you see that film *The Arm Wrestler from Solitude*? I can just imagine it. Living with a lot of people on a farm like that, working in the forestry sector. Being far away from everything but in a house full of life and aunts and uncles and children and friends and everything.

This is productive forest too, I say. You could always work here.

This is a wimpy forest, Tove says.

Wimpy? Wimpy, is it? It's just like any other forest.

She laughs.

Okay. But it's still a little tame.

Oh, but you see, it's constantly changing. This area, for example, I signal widely with my arms, this was dense spruce forest last spring. And look at it now: it's all cleared, all that's left is just this little clump of trees. And the forest there on the other side – half of the trees came down in that storm, what was it called, Sven. And the gravel pit. I'll show you the gravel pit. Once you've seen it, just wait.

Tove puts her arm around my waist.

Okay, she says.

We have midsummer dinner under the big sun umbrella and the rain is falling quietly around us. Tove is telling us about people she knows and the things they do and say; there are always so many new names in her stories. Disillusioned, they are all disillusioned, every one of them, she says – all her friends in Malmö. But even so, she says, something is going to happen, maybe not now, but one day. One day we'll come up with something new. A life.

We sing. Old songs which Martina and Tove learned as children. Songs about the pike in the reeds or the long road home in the autumn. Martina rolls a joint from the scraps in her sachet. She lights it, blowing the smoke out into the rain.

I reach my hand across to someone and find I'm grabbing hold of the large, cool feather duvet. I open my eyes and screw them up again, move my toes a bit, then my fingers. Martina is sitting in the kitchen stirring her cup of coffee. It's palpable throughout the house: Tove has gone. How could it happen, when did it happen? I didn't think I even fell asleep! I dreamed I was awake and dinner went through the night and into the morning – we were lying on the grass.

Martina gets up. She kisses my forehead, walks into the living room and puts a record on. I stand for a while, staring out of the window. Now the sun is shining as if nothing has happened, all is bright, the garden full of flowers.

Ritve

Inside the tent, I seem to expand. I bought a three-person model so I wouldn't feel too squashed in, but when I go inside my shoulders grow wide, my legs long. They need to be positioned, made room for and shifted around, and then they just get in the way again. The systems for my new existence are under development. Pockets and compartments: the knife goes here, the head torch goes there. I make a real effort. Can't sleep during the day: I lie there with earplugs in, staring into my eye mask. Try to stay awake all night but doze off way too often. *Just stay awake just stay awake just stay awake*, I bite my own hand. Out with the camping stove. Boil boil. A swig of coffee, a smack on the cheek. *Wakey-wakey wakey-wakey*. The forest is murmuring. Where are the wild boar? Not here. Not here. Have they broken camp? Did they get away?

Mia

Is anyone home? Grandad and I are playing. Hello Sigga children, where are you all? They are hiding somewhere in the schoolhouse. The place can't be as empty as this. We can't be so few in number. It's just a matter of looking in the right places. Grandad, you're Ivar Sandberg. No, I'm Ivar Sandberg and the children are hiding. Go and hide, Grandad. I'll go outside and count to a hundred. Okay? Go on and hide.

I stand with my head pressed against the wall of the schoolhouse, slowly counting to ten, twenty, one hundred. Coming, ready or not. Hello children, COMING, READY OR NOT! I sneak across the veranda, in through the door, down the corridor, open the door to the big hall, slowly does it. Standing in the middle of the floor is Grandad, where I left him. Grandad, I say, you're meant to go and hide. Hello! Do you hear me? How am I supposed to find you when you're just standing there? I say it in Ivar Sandberg's voice. Now I'm going back outside to count to two hundred, I say. While I'm counting you're to go and hide. You have plenty of time. Okay? I'm going now.

I count. I wait with my head against the wall. Shit. Shit, I can't do this anymore. What am I playing at? What am I playing at! I miss Sara. I want to go home. I can't go home. I want to go home. Nothing's going to happen here. Nothing's going to happen! He's old now, he got old, he was never my age. He wasn't my friend, my sister, my brother. He was no parent, he was always old, old boy, he must be allowed to die if that's what he's supposed to do. I'll go home. Move back in with Sara. We can forget it all. Put Grandad somewhere. With clean sheets and friendly staff. Visit him once a week. Leave the Sigga children alone. Leave Grandad to fade away like old people do. I am not a Sigga child. I'll go home.

I go back in. There is Grandad, quietly watching me, so small in the big, bright room.

Ritve

I open the zip of the tent and lift my legs out. I sit, staring at the treetops. Yet another day and I've lost count. I brush my teeth, sit down on a stump and write to Zoya. I'm an inexperienced letter writer, I don't know where to start. I'm sitting on a stump, I write, camping out now, in Småland. My handwriting is childish and my senses are hazy – what shall I tell her about the scenery? I try to sharpen my focus, try to listen, but nothing stands out clearly. I'm short of the sleep that makes me receptive. I don't have anything to tell. A breeze in the trees, a light slumber without dreams, which left me dry and empty. Is this all there is?

No, something will happen today. I fold the letter up, tucking it in my backpack. I pack a day bag and head off due west with a compass around my neck. Many kilometres away from the tent, I see a hunter. He's sitting up in his lookout tower, young and wiry. I stop in front of the tower. He looks out, he says: Aha, out for a walk, are you? You're disrupting my sound field, clomping in like that. His hearing is extraordinary, he tells me, he sits for hours, concentrating. Once he is exposed to the entire sound field, he is able to hear the wild boar from many kilometres away. He has been aware of me approaching for a long time, he says, my footsteps have distracted him.

He nods at me.

Fancy coming up?

I climb the ladder and squat beside him in the tower.

He holds out a hand.

Volt, he says, Protection Hunter.

Oh I see, I say, what are you protecting?

Our area! There are lots of us this year, he says, people stand by one another here, where we have been hit the hardest. We pull together. The Hunt Strategists do the analysing. And the Protection Hunters are prepared throughout the year.

He takes his cap off.

I look out into the trees.

The tower isn't high but I'd still expected some kind of view. It looks the same as being on the ground.

I say, You can't see anything from up here.

Oh come on, Volt says, the point is that they can't see us.

They do see the tower though? I say.

Nope, he says, they think it's a tree.

I frown. They don't think that.

He shrugs.

Or they have a death wish, for all I know, he sneers. They come anyway.

He gives me a furtive sideways glance.

Yup. Every night. And you should see the sows. Big as fuck. Meat to feed a whole army.

Oh right, I say, so what do you do with it? Eat it all yourself?

Hell, no. I don't like meat. I give it to my old man. I'm only a Protection Hunter.

He observes me silently.

You out hunting too?

Something like that, I say.

In a tower?

In a tent.

Well, well, he nods, sounds exciting. He looks at me for a long time, says, Just don't get too close, if you see what I'm saying. I'm protecting this part of the forest.

Are there any other badly affected areas nearby? I say.

They all are, says Volt, lowering his voice. It's war. The new generation is out for revenge. We took their ancestors. It wasn't pretty, it was just for the meat in those days.

He looks me in the eyes.

I just want to do my bit, you see. So people's fields are left alone.

Could I film you? I say.

What was that? Volt says.

Could I film you? Just do a short interview. About your work.

No bloody way! I don't want anyone recognising me.

You can sit with your back to me if you want, I say. And I can use a voice changer. They're very good.

I said no, says Volt. He tosses his head back. I'm not going to be filmed by anyone!

No, okay.

I lean against the frame of the tower, trying to take in the view. It's difficult to see what distinguishes this place from all the others in the forest, why the wild boar would thrive so well here of all places. Scattered pines, rocks, ferns, grass. No obvious tracks. I crane my head around and study the construction. The tower is homelier than others I've seen; we're sitting on a raised area and above us is a little room with windows on all sides.

So this is your place, I say.

Volt nods. You could say that. At certain times of the year. He smiles at me. Yeah, it's pretty nifty, huh.

Do you sleep during the day? I say.

He looks intently at me. Does it look like I sleep? I don't have time to, I'm on the job around the clock.

But they don't appear during the day, I try.

No, but I have to guard the tower, he says. Anyone could take my place if I end up nodding off. Loads of people are after my job. What you see here is the prime location – he draws an outline with his arm, the most solidly built tower in the area, in the best position. I spent weeks scouting out the right spot. I was in the forest, listening out like fucking crazy every night.

Volt opens a juice.

The sun is taking the chill off.

We sit, looking out into the woods.

Okay, he says, let me give you a little tip. Between colleagues.

He takes a swig from the bottle.

The new generation, he says, they like sugary stuff. Sweets and doughnuts. Anything with icing. Over there, he points, you see. Their feeding place. Other people bugger about with potatoes and old kitchen scraps. They don't realise that the pigs have grown picky. Just like us. Who wants old spuds when you can have pastries?

Their feeding place. I try to picture it, the wild boar coming to scoff doughnuts and sweets while I'm lying on my stomach in the tent extension, filming. I have to try hard to see it. This really isn't how I had imagined things.

Mia

The sun wakes me up.

I find Grandad in the big hall: he is sitting on the chair, waiting.

Hi, I say. We're going home today. I take his hand and squeeze it. Are you ready?

He stares into the wall.

Did you hear me, I say, we're going home. I tug a little at his arm. We should pack.

He doesn't move.

Grandad, I say. We should pack.

He looks at me.

I pull at his arm.

Come on.

He pulls back.

I see.

I let go of his arm and sit on the floor.

Okay. So, what are we to do? We can't go on like this, can we now? I thought you'd like being here. But you don't want to do anything. Do you know where we are? Do you know this is Siggalycke? Huh?

We look one another in the eyes for a long time. He seems angry.

What do you want? Shall we play something else? Fancy that?

His face is unchanged.

Okay, I say. How about a role-playing game?

I get up.

This is what we'll do.

You can stay where you are.

That's it.

This is a new game.

Now we'll act out the story, just the way you told it, okay?

We recreate a classroom, Grandad and I.

Not Ivar Sandberg's – this is a different classroom. The one that came afterwards, when Ivar Sandberg went, leaving the Sigga children to Bengt-Åke Berg.

Grandad is sitting on the chair, playing himself.

I'm playing all the other roles.

We have morning assembly.

The first morning assembly with Bengt-Åke Berg.

Grandad is sitting at his desk. He misses Ivar Sandberg.

He is chewing his fingers.

Bengt-Åke Berg stands at his teacher's desk, looking out across the children.

He lowers his eyes and clasps his hands.

Our Father who art in Heaven.

Grandad looks out through the window.

We have football.

Grandad has hidden behind the spruce trees.

Bengt-Åke Berg doesn't know all their names yet, but he is counting.

Ah, yes, someone is missing, someone who doesn't want to play with the others!

Time to send out a search party. Prize for the one who finds him!

Oskar Jönsson gets a hymn book.

Grandad is lying on his stomach in the big hall.

Bengt-Åke Berg is outside collecting spruce twigs in the hedge.

We have chemistry.

Grandad is lying on his back in the big hall.

He has a wet handkerchief over his mouth and nose.

The other children circle around him.

We call this ether, says Bengt-Åke Berg.

Oskar Jönsson is poking Grandad with his index finger.

Bengt-Åke Berg is writing on the board.
$(C_2H_5)_2O$.
Just watch this.

Grandad has packed his things and headed out.

He's still exhausted after the chemistry experiment, but he's on his way. He's walking through the forest towards Tingsryd, to where Ivar Sandberg has moved. Grandad has decided he will ask at every house in Tingsryd. He will find Ivar Sandberg if it's the last thing he does.

It is autumn, almost November. The trees are bare and there are no animals in this forest, no one keeping him company.

He's walking towards Tingsryd; he walks all night until he falls into the brook. When he gets out his legs are so frozen he can't walk any further. He lies in the moss, crying. Then he stops crying. He's just silent. He thinks: I am dead.

No! Grandad shouts. He shouts it in my voice. No! That's not how it went. I didn't die. I walked on. Surely you can see that! I didn't die. Now listen. This is what happened. He takes the tape recorder out of my hand.

Glenn

I'm woken in the middle of the night and think it must be the wild boar again, sneaking about outside, and I go to the window. I wait there, keeping watch, and when nothing happens I go downstairs and out to the lawn. I listen. I wonder if it's a hangover giving me a queasy stomach; I sit down on the steps, rocking back and forth. Out here it's quiet – there are no sounds from the forest, just a dull murmur of leaves and branches. A light comes on in the kitchen, yellow and bright against the watery light out here. I see Martina in the window, moving around in the kitchen, opening cupboards and drawers. My mouth is dry, I cough up beer and phlegm. Martina comes outside and sits down next to me. The sky is light blue but we can see aircraft and satellites passing over our heads. I want food, a spread of savoury dishes, a robust wine from the cellar. A night that never ends. Shall we call in sick tomorrow? I whisper. Martina leans in closer, nodding.

Martina's alarm goes off and she gets up. She'll go to work again as if nothing happened. I'm cold, Martina come here, you're sick like me, come back. Sorry, she says, and walks around the room putting her clothes on. Sorry, I'd forgotten, I've got a new client today, I have to be there. She brushes her hair in a rush. But you stay in bed, I'll bring us back a takeaway. She kisses my feet and pulls a sweater on. What do you want? She puts on her lipstick. I don't know, I say. I roll over to her side of the bed. Once she's left, I get out of bed and call work, tell them I'm sick, then pull the covers over me.

I wake up hungry and cook up some pasta. Is it still morning? Afternoon? I check my emails. Tove has written: she's back in Malmö, she couldn't stay in Småland any longer. She couldn't go to Norrland either. Maybe she'll stay in Malmö, maybe she'll go on somewhere. Nothing is certain. She was pleased to see us, she writes, but she also felt detached, unfamiliar, mournful during her visit. *I don't know any more if you're joking when you talk about the Ice Age,* she writes, *but it makes me frustrated. I don't understand why you can't let it go. There really isn't going to be an Ice Age, there isn't going to be a fucking Ice Age and you know that too.* I sign out. My mind is blank. Back to bed, the saucepan beside me, the bottle of ketchup on the bedside table. I'm in a cold sweat, eat too quickly, listen to the sports bulletin on the radio. The macaroni slides easily into my stomach. IFK Gothenburg are one-nil down to Djurgården. I look up out of the window.

I'm not in the mood for anything. I don't want to lie here, don't want to get up, don't want to sleep. But the easiest thing is just to stay in bed.

When I wake up again it's half past seven and I can hear the rain. The room is hot and humid. I'm up out of bed and look outside. Martina's car is parked in its usual place. And over there, behind the currant bushes, the wild boar have gathered. Now there are twice as many as last time, squeezed together with their snouts in the earth, the striped boarlets in the middle. Their tails wagging. I wait. Once they have shambled their way past I hurry downstairs, wanting to get outside and inspect. Here I am, in the exact spot where they were gathered, my socks soaking up rain from the grass. I'm aggravated by the damage, it's worse than I'd expected, but I'm also exhilarated. I call out to Martina. She's had a long day and rests her head on my shoulder. We stand like that for a while, with the rain falling on us.

What are we supposed to do? says Martina.

Nothing, I say. We'll wait and see.

She raises her head. Her hair has gone lank and flat in the rain.

Do you think they'll be back? she says.

I've seen them before, I say.

Me too, she says. A few times.

I thought wild boar were timid, I say.

Perhaps we'll have to put a fence up, says Martina.

They know how to climb, I say.

Martina sighs, smiles wearily at me. I'm going inside, she says. I bought falafel.

I stay there for a while looking out at the garden. I take my wet socks off and hang them on a branch of the currant bush.

Ritve

Maybe they have been here, the wild boar; now they are somewhere else. And as they go from one place to another, so must I. I pack up my tent and brush life back into the blades of grass that have faded beneath it. I go via Gittan's house and fill my jerry can with water.

Did you get anything on film then? she asks. Besides me?

No, I say, not yet, but your part was good.

Pah! she says. Come in so we can chat. You'll want a cup of something.

It's a great relief to take my boots off. My sweat-soaked socks are grubby and discoloured and they leave marks behind when I cross the parquet. She serves coffee at the veranda table and pours liquorice into a bowl.

They were here overnight, she says. The animals. I'll show you.

She drops sugar cubes into her cup and stirs.

Biggan, my sister, she's very worried. She's not

sleeping – I can hear her at night, she goes outside to chase them away. She doesn't want to talk about it when I ask. No, you see, she says I'm raving, but I've seen her through the window.

Gittan slurps her coffee, shaking her head. No, this can't just go on and on, she says.

What are you going to do? I ask.

Well, what *can* we do, she says. Hunt them down? No, I don't feel like any of that. Biggan, she used to hunt a lot when she was young. But I don't know, there are so many protection hunters here nowadays. You can hardly go into the forest without coming across them.

I nod. I met one myself, I say. He says he fires his gun every night.

Well, we'll just have to see, says Gittan. She sits back into her chair, watching out of the window.

Look, she says after a while, rain clouds. Really dark ones. We'd better go out, before it starts pouring.

We just make it out to the wheat fields, looking over the crops, when the heavens open. Gittan holds her coat over both of us. This whole area, she says, tracing it with her hand. Just look at it! The fields spread out in all directions and the wild boar have carved paths right through the wheat, eating and trampling their way across the farmland. There's a crash of thunder in the distance, and then the rain eases. We head indoors. I gather my things together and put my damp coat on. Back inside I notice my stink. Not wanting to give Gittan a hug, I offer my hand. Such formalities, she says. Come here! She squeezes her little body against mine.

The sky clears up towards evening. The forest is glistening. Water from the trees drips onto my forehead and I walk until I come to a lake, where I throw my bag onto the shore. Someone has painstakingly prepared a fire pit made up of large and small stones supporting each other. There are logs in the centre, semi-charred; all wood in the forest is damp. But the fire does take – it crackles and hisses and I keep it going with air and notepaper. And everything dries. I cook my last packet of instant soup. Mushroom and chive. I let it thicken and season it with the moist salt. I open out my map. This could be Sandsjön, the lake that goes all the way to Konga.

I collect my things and follow the shoreline for as long as the ground allows. It turns into reeds and wetland and I walk into the forest. The main path comes to the public highway and, on the other side, a plant nursery extends over the slopes. The working day is over and the pines and spruce are enclosed in their incubators. They are much smaller than I am, for now. I could so easily smash the glass and kill them with my bare hands. Pull them out of the ground and spread them all over the slope, watch the sun come out and fry them. But I don't; I sit down close to them in front of the glass, singing a lullaby. My voice sounds low and hoarse, unfamiliar, beautiful.

I climb into a tractor and sit back against the leather. This is a good place to be; I kick the mud off my boots and whistle. Shielded by the tractor's sides and windows, I stare at the sky and my solitude surprises me. I long for home. It doesn't do to be alone here; there's no space for it in the woods. The trees are reliable company, cradling and reassuring, saturating me. I used to think the damp, dense forest would connect me with all living things, but I have no sense of sharing this forest with the wild boar. I don't feel their movements, I don't know what they want. Maybe they just want large numbers. Reproduction. Suddenly I remember I didn't come to be alone. It was something else, something familiar that I felt a yearning for. Now I'm here, I don't know how to be alone in the forest. It was by the sea that I learned to be alone, standing outside on the headland, shrieking at the birds. They never became my friends – I quickly stopped performing tricks for them, trying to impress them. I would shriek like they did, not to be like them, but to show I could manage alone, and as my lungs were bigger I would shriek louder than they did.

In the tractor the sense of loneliness is greater than in the tent but I'm too tired, too tired to put the tent up. I wrap myself up in my raincoat and sigh. The sun is orange, I can't blink.

I wake up to the rain, morning rain on the roof of the tractor. And in through the window. It's slightly open and my shoulder is cold and wet. The plant nursery is a lake of mud. I open the door and jump out into the lake. Brown water flows around my boots. I wait for a while, summoning courage for the day ahead. A human standing on the other side of the lake begins to move towards me through the mud, saying: Hello there, how's it going, are you looking for something? I shake my head but the human comes nearer, and closer still, continuing to talk to me, pointing towards a building: We're about to have breakfast in there with the gang now. Are you coming? You can't just stay out here all morning. Okay, I say. I take my bag. The human's name is Mika. Mika says: Close the window, who's left it open all night?

We wade our way through the mud. Mika opens the door for me and we step inside with our boots on. The others are sitting around the table but their boots are on too; the floor is caked in mud and we remove our coats, pour coffee. I'm tired and hungry. I sit at the table with Mika and the others. People are sleepy and not saying very much; they smile a little at me, serve more coffee into their mugs, muttering over the top of each other. We eat coarse rye bread with pickled cucumber and cheese. Mika goes outside to smoke.

Their break is over and it just keeps raining. They don their overalls, sigh and laugh, pat me on the shoulder: You can sit here and warm yourself up, take it easy. They go outside. I stay indoors watching them; the tractors start moving across the open fields straight away. No, I'm not finished! It's not enough. I can't stay here. I put my coat back on, shove the door open. I wade through the mud to a tractor that hasn't moved off yet, knocking on the window. I call to the person inside – Hello there, do you know anything about the wild boar? He opens the door and looks out.

What are you on about?

I say it clearly: Do you know anything about the wild boar? Where are they?

The man sitting at the wheel squints at me through the raindrops. Everywhere, he says. They're everywhere! He turns away, tries to close the door. I hold it open.

Hang on, I can't find them!

He starts the tractor up, yelling through the din: I have work to do, you know!

I've got work to do too, I say. I can't wait any more.

What are you on about? he shouts.

I can't wait any more! I shout.

I'm shaking in frustration. His face changes, he

looks at me aghast, turning off the engine. Okay, okay, he says. What do you want? I pull my hood down.

Can you just tell me where they are? I say. He throws his hands up.

I don't know, he says. Ask someone else. Ask the hunt strategists! Or what's his name, Arnold, the man who makes the films, he lives in Hornanäs. Ask him! Bloody hell, you're soaked through. Go inside for a bit. Have a sandwich or something. Wild boar don't come out in this weather. Okay?

I let go of the door and he shuts it, smiles and raises his hand up towards me, drives out across the mud, waves swelling behind the tractor. And I run. As fast as I can, past the nursery building and down the slope again, onto the road and into the forest, throwing myself down into the moss. With my fingers wet, I unfold the tent, fastening it with pegs. I tighten and knot and adjust, pushing the pegs into the earth. There we are, and it has never looked better! I hang my coat up in the tent extension, crawl inside, empty my dripping backpack onto the floor. Everything inside it is dry, even my feet in my boots are dry – they smell musty, but they're dry. I pull all my clothes off and spread them over the floor, lying across them on my belly. I take short, irregular breaths, feel my heart beating against the ground. I lie still until my breathing finds a rhythm. I stretch my arms out, swim great strokes through my clothes, greater and greater strokes and my clothes float, I float, leaving a swell behind me. I propel my way along ever more rapidly, steam coming off me, heating up the tent which starts to billow in the moisture, and the steam settles on the tent fabric. The canvas gets soggy with steam, the steam turns into hot liquid and starts running down the sides of the tent, dropping onto me from the ceiling, and I sink, heavily, down towards the bottom.

Recollections of a Sigga Child

Chapter one. The door creaks. A window frame taps against the wall of the schoolhouse. The light falls across an empty classroom. The breeze is balmy. It's still silent. But wait. If you're really quiet, you'll soon hear the clatter of little feet on the floor. Shhh. They're coming. There I am, it's my breathing you can hear. It's 1938. It's my first day at school. Today is the first of August –

Grandad!

The first of August and I have stepped inside the school hall. I will –

Grandad!

Ah, that's my grandchild calling me. One moment.

Grandad, come on!

I can't play now.

But I've got something to say.

Not now, Mia, I'm busy with the equipment here.

But I've got something to say! Sigga's outside.

Who?

Sigga. The wild boar!

What wild boar? Mia, it's 1938. There aren't any wild boar in Småland, that's an anachronism.

She's outside! Come and see.

Please, Mia, the wild boar only escaped in the forties. They're enclosed in fences a long way from here. Off you go.

But come and take a look!

I don't have time. I'm telling the story about my first day at school, it's important, I don't have much time left.

But I've heard it. We've all heard it.

It's for the sound archive! Out you go now.

But she's on the grass, looking at me. She's just there!

Go and play in the kitchen. Close the door.

Right. Excuse the interruption. Where were we? It was – oh yes. I'm sitting still at my desk. My heart is pounding. I see him for the first time. Ivar Sandberg! He's standing behind the teacher's desk. His look is serious but friendly. Our legs are tingling. Dear children, says Ivar Sandberg. His voice is warm and confident. Welcome to Siggalycke. This is where you'll be spending the next seven years of your lives. Writing, counting, and, most of all, learning. The world out there is cold and hostile. We're living in uneasy times. But here, at Siggalycke, you're safe. The school floor will support you, its walls will protect you from evil. As of today, I hereby call you my Sigga children.

Glenn

The last day at work before the holidays, I'm in no hurry to get home. We've closed the office and most people have left, it's just me and Torgny still around. It's nice being here, doing nothing, just taking my time. I drink my coffee slowly, slurping. I click on a few pages here and there, write a rather clever out-off-office email response. Torgny knocks at my door.

Have a lovely holiday, Glenn! Up to much?

Well, I say, I reckon I'm going to be at home mostly. Taking things easy. Tidying up odds and ends in the garden.

Splendid, he says. Have a good one then – he raises his hand to bid farewell.

I sign out and remain where I am, staring at the monitor until the screensaver comes on. The space opens out. Shapes emerge on the screen. Switching from blue to purple, purple to yellow, green, blue, purple again. I trace the little movements with my eyes. The shapes give birth to one another, mutate, so many colours, so many forms. So wild, dazzling, constantly in transformation.

Recollections of a Sigga Child

Chapter two. I used to love botany lessons. That was where he could really –

I'll just borrow this a minute.

No. Mia, what are you doing, give it to me.

I just want to tell a little story!

Mia. Give the equipment back. Go out now and play. I've not finished.

I want to tell a story as well.

No, this is for the local heritage museum. That's why we came here. It's about the Sigga children now. It has to be historically relevant.

But I know how things used to be!

That's enough now. You are a child! You should listen to me. I'm the only one you have now, Mia. I'm going to die soon and then you'll have no one. Make the most of every second with me. Do you understand? Every second!

I've got Sara.

Not anymore.

I've got Sara.

She left you. You chose me.

You're lying! I didn't choose you!

Just you wait. I'll die soon and then you'll have no one.

Recollections of a Sigga Child

Chapter two. New attempt.

Ah-he-mm.

I used to love botany lessons. Ivar Sandberg made them magical. He – he –

Ah-he-mm.

Recollections of a Sigga – a Sigga child. Chapter two. I used to love botany lessons! Ivar Sandberg made them so magical. We would go out into the forest, all the Sigga children hand in hand, under his wing, and – and – it was magical, under his wing, we went into the forest, hand in hand, all the children, and we – and it was – and we – all the Sigga children – under his wing – all children were – we were – pardon me – I can't – yes I can – it was – yes I can – we went into the forest, all the Sigga children together, hand in hand we went, with – with Ivar Sandberg looking out for us, ahead of us, he told us about – it was a flower called – it was called – it had the most beautiful name – it was called – it was called – what was it – Mia! Where are you? Can you help, Mia? Come here! What was the flower called? Can you hear me? My sweet Sigga child, come here!

Ritve

I keep the tent up, leaving things where they are; I take my wallet and coat and walk along to the road. All my food has run out – I ate wood sorrel for breakfast. It gave a pleasant burning sensation in my empty stomach. I walk down the road to Tingsryd, sticking my thumb out as cars drive past. I get pretty much halfway when one of them stops. Glenn isn't going my way beyond Tingsryd, but he'll drive me right to Börjes department store. He comes into the shop with me, seeing as he's here anyway. I opt for crisps and coffee and garlic from the shelves, a lot of tomato soup and noodles and chocolate. Glenn goes for cheese and wheat flour, and we wait in the queue together. I'll probably light the oven tonight, he says. Our pizza oven, we've got one, you see.

There's a lake close to the store. I watch Glenn's car pull away and sit to rest for a while on the shore.

A red Ford brakes heavily, and Per Anders waves from the driver's seat. I'm so happy to see him, happy to be in his car while the forest swishes past with no time for my eyes to fix on anything.

What brings you out here? he says.

I've been stocking up, I say.

Right, yes, he says, I can see that. Aren't you going to Arnold's? He's having a barbeque tonight. Nothing fancy, but lovely people. Cracking stories. You must have a fair few yourself! Won't you be there?

Oh, I'll be making dinner at home, I say. Maybe some other day.

Yes, okay, well, it's not like it'll be the last time, I suppose. We usually – what's all this?

Per Anders slows down. On the road ahead of us there's a parked car, to the left of it another car smashed into a tree, its bonnet buckled and windscreen shattered.

We park on the road verge.

Bloody hell, says Per Anders. The bloke from Malmö, that's *his* car.

We get out.

What happened?

Two people are smoking.

Wild boar, says the first one. They came running along this way, right here, she points. The guy swerved and crashed into the trees. There were loads of them, absolutely loads.

We saw it, says the other one. We were coming from the other direction. They took him to Växjö. Didn't look good, not good at all.

Where are –

I clear my throat.

Where are the wild boar?

The first one stubs her cigarette out on the tarmac.

Must've come out of it okay.

I stare at the car, crumpled into the tree. It takes a while before I recognise it.

Mia

We are standing on the grass. We have packed our things, our cases are ready in the hall. Our bodies spindly, our hair close-cropped, we are completely silent this evening. A cool breeze blows, making the fine hairs on the back of my neck stand on end. There is the apple tree. There he sits, Ivar Sandberg. There is Sigga, lying next to him. They appear as silhouettes against the sky. We've been looking at them for a long time, waiting. Watched the sun go down and the twilight fall. We've let the insects crawl over our feet and into our ears. We wait. The mosquitoes swarm, moving in great clouds above our heads. A car drives past on the road, followed by another. Now Sigga lifts her head. They lean closer to each other. Ivar Sandberg nods towards her. There's a rustle in the trees. I can't hear what they're saying, but I can see their mouths moving.

Ritve

I walk back to the tent a different way, through a part of the forest I don't recognise. I navigate via the brook, which snakes around, becomes small and narrow, then widens again, rushing over the rocks. The route is demanding – there is no order here. Storm-toppled trees have come down in all directions and the forest is taking shape over the trunks in new ways, fresh growth taking detours, living trees growing on top of dead ones.

Inside the tent I lie awake on my back, my arms stretched out wide. I look up at the canvas ceiling rippling lightly in the breeze. I am awake, I am dreaming. I am imagining the future. It's been a long while since I thought about it, thinking beyond a day or a week at a time. The future, it looks something like this. Out of the forest of Småland a sea is born, a different sea. This isn't the Baltic. It's greater, so infinitely greater, a salty ocean and a shoreline covered with bladderwrack and rocks. No houses, no trees to be seen, just rocks.

Large ones, flat ones, bright, light red ones. The wild boar are right next to me with their snouts in the air. We shut our eyes and jump into the waves. We swim all evening, collect seaweed, large clumps of it which we dry over a fire. We settle down around the flames, staring into the embers, growing quieter and more restful during the night. My hair has dried, as have the coats on the wild boar. The breeze is warm, we sleep under open skies, we live on seaweed and saltwater all summer long.

ACKNOWLEDGEMENTS

The quotations on pages 15, 29 and 30 are taken from the movie *My Winnipeg* (2007) and included with the kind permission of its writer Guy Maddin and Coach House Books, who published the script in 2009.

The poem quoted on page 32 is from 'Nothing' from *The Land That Is Not* (1925) by Edith Södergran, translated from the Swedish by Andy Turner.

The illustration used on the cover and as vignettes throughout interiors is *Vieux Chênes au Bas-Bréau*, by Adolphe Théodore Jules Martial Potémont. Photo by Birmingham Museums Trust, licensed under CC0.

ABOUT THE AUTHOR

Hannah Lutz was born in 1984 and grew up in Ekenäs, in southern Finland. She has an MA from Finland's Åbo Akademi University. She later moved to Denmark and attended the Writing School in Copenhagen. Still based in Denmark, she lives just outside Roskilde.

Her short story 'Den elfte versionen' / 'The Eleventh Version' won the Umeå Short Story Award, Sweden, in 2011.

Vildsvin / Wild Boar is Lutz's debut novel. Written in Swedish, it was first published as the Danish translation in 2016 by Rosinante in Denmark; the original Swedish text was first published in 2017 by Förlaget in Finland and Albert Bonniers Förlag in Sweden.

Her second novel, *Selma*, was published by Förlaget in Finland in 2023.

ABOUT THE TRANSLATOR

Andy Turner is a writer, reviewer, translator, and former school teacher and examiner. He works with both Swedish and German and is a member of SELTA and the Translators Association of the Society of Authors.

He graduated with an MA in Literary Translation from the University of East Anglia in 2017. He was Swedish mentee in the 2018-19 National Centre for Writing's Emerging Literary Translator Mentorships Programme, working alongside Sarah Death.

His translation of *Wild Boar* is his first full-length adult translation publication.

ABOUT THE EMMA PRESS

The Emma Press is an independent publishing house based in Birmingham. It was founded in 2012 by Emma Dai'an Wright and has grown to five part-time staff members following support from Arts Council England's Elevate programme in 2020-23.

The Emma Press specialises in poetry, short fiction and children's books, with translations across all genres. Recent publications have won the Michael Marks Illustration Award and been shortlisted for the CLiPPA and the Week Junior Book Awards.

In 2024 The Emma Press was a Regional Finalist for Small Press of the Year Award in the British Book Awards, as well as shortlisted for the Independent Publishers Guild's Alison Morrison Diversity, Equity & Inclusion Award.

The Emma Press is passionate about publishing literature which is welcoming and accessible

theemmapress.com
@TheEmmaPress

MORE FROM THE EMMA PRESS

ESSAY COLLECTIONS

Bound: A Memoir of Making and Remaking, by Maddie Ballard
How Kyoto Breaks Your Heart, by Florentyna Leow
Tiny Moons: A Year of Eating in Shanghai, by Nina Mingya Powles

SHORT STORY COLLECTIONS

About Us, by Reda Gaudiamo, translated from Indonesian by Ikhda Ayuning Maharsi Degoul and Phillipa Barker
Parables, Fables, Nightmares, by Malachi McIntosh
Blood & Cord: Writers on Early Parenthood, edited by Abi Curtis

POETRY COLLECTIONS

Daughter of the Sun, by Rachel Spence
Europe, Love Me Back, by Rakhshan Rizwan

POETRY PAMPHLETS

After the Rites and Sandwiches, by Kathy Pimlott
Mother Night, by Serge ♆ Neptune
In the Name of Red, by Z. R. Ghani
Makeover, by Laurie Bolger

BOOKS FOR CHILDREN

Please Don't Read The Footnotes Please, by Rob Walton
The Skeleton in the Cupboard, by Lilija Berzinska, translated from Latvian by Žanete Vēvere Pasqualini and Sara Smith
The Untameables, by Clare Pollard, illus. by Reena Makwana